Juggling Jinx

"Brian, could you practice your juggling act?" Mrs. McKenna asked. "Just do the rings. We don't have time for anything else."

Brian Mueller took the colorful rings from his backpack and went up onto the auditorium stage.

"I'm all ready," he said. He held the rings in front of him and prepared to toss them into the air. "Now for my first—aaaargh!"

All of a sudden, Brian's feet went out from under him. He flew through the air. Then he landed on the stage with a loud thud!

Books in the New Bobbsey Twins™ Series

Available from MINSTREL Books

BOBBSEY T?W•i•N•S™

#29

The Case of the Tricky Trickster

LAURA LEE HOPE

Illustrated by

DAVID F. HENDERSON

A MINSTREL® BOOK

PUBLISHED BY POCKET BOOKS

New York   London   Toronto   Sydney   Tokyo   Singapore

A MINSTREL PAPERBACK *ORIGINAL*

A Minstrel Book published by
POCKET BOOKS, a division of Simon & Schuster Inc.
1230 Avenue of the Americas, New York, NY 10020

Copyright © 1992 by Simon & Schuster Inc.
Produced by Mega-Books of New York, Inc.

ISBN: 0-671-73041-X

First Minstrel Books printing April 1992

10 9 8 7 6 5 4 3 2 1

THE NEW BOBBSEY TWINS is a trademark of
Simon & Schuster Inc.

THE BOBBSEY TWINS, A MINSTREL BOOK, and colophon are
registered trademarks of Simon & Schuster Inc.

Cover art by Dominick Finelle

Printed in the U.S.A.

Contents

The Case
of the
Tricky
Trickster

1

On with the Show!

"Wow! Check out those tap dancers from Mrs. Ellsworth's class," Flossie Bobbsey said to her twin brother, Freddie.

Freddie peeked through the curtain. "They're really good," he agreed.

"My juggling act is a lot better than that," said Brian Mueller. He was in Freddie and Flossie's class, and he liked to brag.

The twins and Brian were standing backstage with a lot of other kids in the Lakeport Elementary School auditorium. It was Wednesday, and they were waiting to practice their parts in the upcoming PTA Variety Show. The show was on

Friday. Freddie and Flossie were going to help their friend Teddy Blake with his magic act.

"Freddie knows how to juggle," Flossie told Brian. "He's really good, too."

"Maybe," Brian said with a shrug. "But not as good as me, I bet."

Out front, Mrs. McKenna, the music teacher, struck a final chord on the piano. The dancers all fell on one knee, their hands in the air.

"Girls, you were wonderful!" shouted Mrs. McKenna. She was also the director of the show. "Now make a straight line, and take a big bow."

"Okay, Flossie, we're next." Freddie picked up a small black box from the floor. "You take the wand and the tablecloth, okay?"

"Okay." Flossie quickly fluffed her curly blond hair.

Mr. Horton, the fifth-grade teacher, stepped onto the stage. He was helping Mrs. McKenna with the show. "Now it's magic time with the amazing Teddy Blake!" he announced. Then he went back behind the curtain.

Flossie and Freddie hurried onstage as Teddy

entered from the other side. Teddy tipped his black top hat to the imaginary audience. Flossie ran over and handed him the thin black wand.

"Thank you, everyone! Thank you!" Teddy told the empty auditorium. "Mind if I remove my hat?"

He took off his hat and tapped it with the wand. "Presto!" he said. Out popped a bunch of paper flowers.

Teddy handed the flowers to Flossie and took a little bow. Then he walked over to Freddie.

"Excuse me," Teddy said loudly. "But you have some coins in your ear." He tapped Freddie's ear, and three quarters fell to the floor.

Freddie quickly bent to pick them up. He stuffed the quarters in his pocket as Teddy walked back to Flossie. Teddy waved his magic wand over Flossie's head. Then he pulled a bright red scarf out of Flossie's ear.

"Great, Teddy!" Mrs. McKenna called out.

For his final trick Teddy asked Flossie to show everyone the empty box that Freddie had brought onstage. "Make sure they get a good

look inside when you walk across the stage," Teddy whispered to Flossie.

Flossie nodded. "Okay," she whispered back.

"Ladies and gentlemen, you see before you an empty box," Teddy told the pretend audience. "Now I will cover the box with this simple silk scarf. And . . ." Teddy tapped the box with his wand. "Presto-chango!" He reached in and pulled out a white teddy bear. "My rabbit is on vacation," he joked.

Mrs. McKenna clapped as Teddy stepped forward to take a big bow. Freddie and Flossie bowed, too.

When the twins stepped offstage with Teddy, they found their older brother and sister waiting for them. Nan and Bert Bobbsey were twelve years old. They were twins, too.

"Great act, you guys," Bert said as Nan nodded in agreement.

Nan turned to Teddy. "How did you make that bear appear?" she asked.

"Sorry," Teddy said with a grin. "Magicians never tell their secrets. And neither do their assistants." He winked at Freddie and Flossie and walked away.

"Are the Aliens going to play in the show?" Flossie asked excitedly when she saw Bert holding his drumsticks. The Aliens were a rock group that Bert and Nan played in.

"Yep. We just found out," Bert told her. "Our school can be part of the show, too. The elementary and middle schools are working together."

"Hey, look who's here," came a familiar voice from behind them. "It's Bert and Nan and the itty-bitty baby Bobbseys."

The voice belonged to Danny Rugg, the biggest bully in Lakeport. He was in Bert and Nan's class at school. He loved to be mean to other kids, especially Freddie and Flossie.

"Buzz off, Danny," Flossie snapped.

Danny pretended to look hurt. "Is that any way to talk to a fellow performer?"

"What are *you* doing in the show, Danny?" Bert asked. "Making bad jokes?"

"Very funny," Danny replied. "It just so happens that I'm playing the accordion."

"You play the accordion?" Flossie asked, giggling.

"I happen to be a musical genius," Danny said.

Bert rolled his eyes. "This I've got to hear."

Mrs. McKenna came up the steps at the side of the stage and looked around. "I think the Aliens should set up their equipment before the show," she told Nan and Bert. "That way you'll be all set to perform when it's your turn."

Nan and Bert went into the wings and hauled their equipment onto the stage. So did Brian Fisher and Jimmy Pendleton, the guitarists in the band.

Mrs. McKenna stepped down off the stage again. "That's fine," she called to the Aliens. "The equipment won't be in the way of the other acts back there."

Just then Mr. Horton walked onto the stage. "Shouldn't we cover it up, at least?" he asked Mrs. McKenna. "We could buy some black cloth."

Mrs. McKenna shook her head. "I don't want

7

to ask the PTA for more money," she replied. "After all, we're supposed to be raising money for *them.*"

"Having equipment onstage during the acts will make us look like a bunch of amateurs," Mr. Horton said. He sounded annoyed.

Mrs. McKenna stared at him. "What's wrong with that, Roy?" she asked. "We *are* a bunch of amateurs."

Mr. Horton didn't answer. He just stalked off into the wings.

Mrs. McKenna picked up her clipboard from the piano and checked the list of performers. "Now, let's see. Who's next?"

"Is it okay if the Aliens set up the drums while the next act rehearses, Mrs. McKenna?" Jimmy asked.

"Of course," the director answered. She looked around. "Is Danny Rugg here?" Danny stepped from behind the curtain at one side of the stage.

"Okay, Danny, you're on," Mrs. McKenna told him. "What song will you be playing?"

Peeking from behind a curtain, Freddie and

Flossie could see Danny's face. He looked embarrassed. " 'When the Swallows Come Back to Capistrano,' " he mumbled.

"Oh, that song was my grandmother's favorite!" Mrs. McKenna said, smiling. "Will you do it for us now, Danny?"

Danny shrugged. "Um, actually, I forgot my accordion."

Mrs. McKenna's smile turned to a frown. "Oh, dear," she said. "Well, please don't forget it next time."

Danny shuffled offstage. "Is Brian Mueller here?" Mrs. McKenna called.

Brian walked slowly onstage, carrying a backpack.

"Brian, you'll be juggling for us, right?" Mrs. McKenna asked.

"You got it," Brian said, unzipping the backpack. He pulled out a few brightly colored balls. "I juggle pins and rings, too," he said.

"Would you like me to play the piano while you juggle?" the director asked.

"I'm going to bring a tape," Brian said. "My dad is making it for me tonight."

"Fine," Mrs. McKenna said. "You can start anytime."

Brian nodded. But as he bent down and pulled three bowling pins out of his pack, he dropped the balls in his arms. The balls began to roll and bounce across the stage.

One of them rolled toward Jimmy, who was unwinding some sound wire. Jimmy picked up the ball and tossed it back to Brian.

Brian tried to catch it but missed. "Oops," he said, chasing the ball to the other side of the stage. Some of the kids who were watching snickered. Mrs. McKenna frowned at them.

At last Brian gathered the balls and pulled three rings from his pack. "I'm ready now," he told Mrs. McKenna. He tossed a ring high into the air. But just as it started coming down, a loud screech filled the auditorium.

2

The Sound of Music

"Yeow!" Brian shouted. He fell to his knees and covered his ears with his hands.

The piercing shriek continued. Bert ran over to one of the Aliens' amplifiers and flipped the power switch. The awful noise stopped.

Brian was still on his knees with his head in his arms. He had been right in front of the speakers, where the noise had come from. Mrs. McKenna ran up the stage steps, and Mr. Horton came rushing over to him.

"Are you all right, Brian?" Mrs. McKenna asked.

Slowly Brian pulled his hands away from his head. "My ears hurt," he said.

"Oh, no," Mrs. McKenna said, biting her lip.

"Well, you'd better get up," Mr. Horton said, pulling Brian to his feet. "You know what real performers say—the show must go on."

Mr. Horton turned to Mrs. McKenna. "I knew it was a bad idea to have that equipment onstage," he told her. Mrs. McKenna looked embarrassed.

Bert was studying the amplifier with a puzzled look.

"What happened?" Freddie asked, walking over to his brother. "Is something broken?"

"That sound was just feedback," Bert explained. "But all the volume controls were on the highest settings. That's really weird. I guess the controls got moved accidentally when we brought the equipment onstage."

"Or maybe someone turned them up on purpose," Freddie suggested. He looked around until he saw Danny Rugg. The older boy was leaning against a wall at one side of the stage. He had a big grin on his face.

"Bert, please be more careful," Mrs. McKenna said. "Loud noises can damage people's hearing."

"Sorry, Mrs. McKenna," Bert said. "It won't happen again."

"Maybe somebody pressed the foot control," Flossie said, coming over with Nan. She pointed to a metal box near the amp. "That could make the volume go up, right?"

"Sure," Nan told her. "But no one was near it."

"Except Brian," Freddie said. He turned to the juggler. "Did you touch that control when you were picking up the balls?"

"Me?" Brian said, looking insulted. "Why would I do something like that? I'm the one who got my ears fried, remember?"

"Let's just be more careful in the future," Mrs. McKenna said. "All of us. Now, can we please clear the stage so Brian can practice his act?"

"I'm feeling kind of weird," Brian said. "Maybe I'd better skip this rehearsal."

"Why don't you sit down for a while and

rest?" Mrs. McKenna suggested. "You might feel better in a few minutes. Let's move on, everyone. Do we have all the Aliens here?"

"We're ready," Nan told her.

Jimmy Pendleton and Brian Fisher picked up their guitars. Bert took his place behind the drums. Nan leaned into the microphone. "One, two, one, two, three!" she chanted. Then the Aliens began to play.

"They're great!" Freddie heard one of the tap dancers say.

Even Mr. Horton started tapping his feet along with the music. At the end of the Aliens' number, all the kids clapped and cheered.

"Fantastic!" Mrs. McKenna called out as she applauded. "Just great!"

Danny Rugg didn't clap. He was still leaning against the wall backstage. "I've heard better music from a chain saw," he told Freddie.

"Maybe you'd like it better if they played it on an accordion," Freddie shot back.

"Why, you little—" Danny began. But just then Mr. Horton came toward them. He tapped Danny on the shoulder.

"I'm looking forward to hearing *you* play, Danny," the teacher said. "Don't forget your instrument next time, okay?" Then he checked the paper in his hand. "Where is Mary Caldera?"

A fifth-grade girl stepped forward. Flossie noticed that her long black hair was a lot curlier than usual. "I'm right here," Mary said. "But my accompanist isn't."

Mr. Horton frowned. "Well, where is she?" he asked.

"Andrea," Mary called over her shoulder. "Come on, it's my turn." A short girl clutching sheet music close to her chest came running up. She looked scared.

"Andrea is playing piano for me," Mary explained.

"Okay," said Mr. Horton. "You two will follow the Aliens. That's not an easy position to be in, but I'm sure you'll do fine."

"Oh, I'm not worried," Mary said, tossing her head. "I'm a very good singer."

"And you're Andrea Lee, correct?" Mr. Horton asked. He checked his list.

"Yes," the girl almost whispered.

"When the Aliens come offstage, Andrea," Mr. Horton told her, "you'll take your place at the piano. Let's try it now."

Andrea walked down the steps and went over to the piano. She sat down and opened her music. With a nervous smile she looked up at the stage, where Mary stood waiting.

"I'm going to sing 'Do-Re-Mi,' from *The Sound of Music,*" Mary announced. She nodded in Andrea's direction. Andrea began to play.

" 'Doe—a deer, a female deer,' " Mary sang loudly.

Flossie, who was standing offstage with Freddie, wrinkled her nose. "She's way off key. That song would be better with just the piano."

Freddie nodded. Then a sudden flash of movement near the ceiling caught his eye. High above the stage was a pole with a large cloth hanging from it.

As Mary reached the next part of her song, the pole started to swing downward. And Mary was right in its path!

3

Wrong Directions

"Mary, look out!" Freddie shouted.

Mary looked up and saw the pole swinging toward her. She let out a shriek and jumped out of the way. The pole didn't hit her, but the cloth slid off and covered her completely.

"Help! I'm caught in this stupid thing!" Mary cried. She waved her arms, trying to get out from under.

Brian Mueller was the first to reach her. "Don't worry, Mary," he said, tugging at the material. "You'll live."

"But my hair!" Mary moaned. "It'll be all messed up!"

Mrs. McKenna and some of the other kids hurried over to help Brian untangle the cloth. When they finally got Mary free, the teacher put her arm around the singer's shoulders. "Mary, are you all right? Can you continue?"

Mary's face was bright red. "Of course not!" she said angrily. "How can I sing when my hair is a mess?"

Mrs. McKenna pressed her lips together. She looked as if she was trying not to laugh.

"I can see that you're very upset, Mary," Mrs. McKenna said. "Why don't you go take care of your hair? Then you'll be able to finish your song."

Freddie looked at Flossie. "Why do you think that pole fell?" he asked her.

"I guess it just came loose," Flossie answered with a shrug.

Freddie pointed toward the ceiling. "See that rope?" he asked. "It was attached to the pole. It goes all the way across the stage and comes down right over there."

Flossie followed Freddie's finger. He was

pointing to the place where Danny Rugg was standing.

"Do you think Danny pulled the rope and made the pole fall?" Flossie asked in a low voice.

"I don't know," Freddie said. "But he *was* standing in the right place to do it."

"But why would Danny want to hurt Mary Caldera?" Flossie asked.

Freddie shrugged. "Why does Danny do any of the dumb things he does? I think we should keep an eye on him from now on."

Just then Freddie and Flossie heard a new voice. "What in the world is going on here?" a woman asked. The twins moved onto the stage and saw a blond woman in a red dress walking down the aisle from the back of the audi-torium.

"Oh, hello, Joy," Mrs. McKenna said. "Everyone, this is Mrs. Franklin, the president of the PTA."

Mrs. Franklin gave them a little wave. "Was that falling curtain part of an act?" she asked Mrs. McKenna.

The director sighed. "I'm afraid not," she

answered. "But don't worry. We'll get everything together by Friday."

"We hope," muttered Mr. Horton, who was now standing behind Mrs. McKenna.

Mrs. McKenna flashed him an angry look. Then she clapped her hands loudly. "All right, everyone," she said. "We have to go on with our rehearsal. I know things seem a little confused. But remember, this is our first run-through. Now, if you're not waiting to perform, please take a seat in the auditorium."

"What about moving that cloth out of the way?" Mr. Horton asked.

"We'll take care of that later," Mrs. McKenna told him.

Mr. Horton frowned as he followed Mrs. McKenna down the steps at the side of the stage. "Next year the PTA should get a real director," he muttered as he passed the twins.

Freddie and Flossie went down the steps, too, and took seats in the auditorium near Bert and Nan. Veronica Freeman came onstage, carrying her violin in one hand and a music stand in the other.

"We need good lighting for her," said Mr. Horton. Then he called out, "Stand in the center of the stage, Veronica." He turned to Mrs. McKenna, who was sitting in the front row, next to Mrs. Franklin. "I want to make sure she can see her music, and that *we* can see her face."

"All right," Mrs. McKenna said. She made a note on her clipboard.

"Veronica, move the music stand about six inches to the left," Mr. Horton told the violin player. "No, no, that's too far. Now bring it about three inches to the right. Hmmm. . . . Maybe if you moved it back a little?"

Freddie saw Mrs. McKenna put her head in her hands. The PTA president got up to go. "Goodbye, Nancy," she told Mrs. McKenna. "And good luck."

Just then Flossie felt a tap on the shoulder. She turned around and saw Teddy Blake in the row behind her. He pulled a deck of cards from his pocket.

"Here, Flossie," he said. "Pick a card. Any card."

Flossie pulled out a card and glanced at it.

"Now slip it back into the deck," Teddy told her. "Anywhere at all."

Flossie put the card back. Other kids gathered around to watch.

Teddy did some complicated moves with the cards. Then he closed his eyes and held the deck against his forehead. "Your card was the seven of hearts," he announced. "Right?"

"I don't remember," Flossie said.

Teddy looked upset.

"Just kidding," Flossie told him with a giggle. "It *was* the seven of hearts. That's a great trick."

Freddie looked back toward the stage. Mr. Horton was still trying to find the right place for Veronica's music stand.

"Can we get on with rehearsal, please?" Mrs. McKenna asked him. "Our time is almost up."

Teddy and the other kids took their seats as Veronica began to play. At first the violin sounded scratchy. But once Veronica warmed up, the music sounded much better.

"Lovely," Mrs. McKenna said when the piece was over. She checked her clipboard. "That's everything for today, except Brian Mueller's juggling act and Danny Rugg's accordion solo."

Mrs. McKenna looked around until she found Brian. He was sitting a few rows behind the twins. "Brian, could you practice your act just once? We still have a few minutes before the after-school buses come."

"Oh, all right," said Brian.

"Just do the rings," Mrs. McKenna told him as he walked toward the stage. "We won't have time for anything else."

Brian took the colorful rings from his backpack and went up the steps.

"Why don't you practice your entrance, too," Mrs. McKenna suggested. "Remember, you'll be following Teddy Blake's magic act."

Brian disappeared backstage for a minute. Then he walked out from behind the curtain. The juggling rings were around his neck.

"I'm all ready," he said, taking the rings off his neck and holding them in front of him as he walked. "Now for my first—aaaargh!"

All of a sudden Brian's feet went out from under him. He flew through the air. Then he landed on the stage with a loud thud.

4

Slipping Up

Mrs. McKenna and Mr. Horton rushed over to Brian. "That was quite a fall," Mrs. McKenna said.

"Are you all right?" Mr. Horton asked. He helped Brian to his feet.

Brian nodded weakly. "I'll be okay."

Mrs. McKenna turned to the kids sitting in the audience. "The rehearsal is over," she announced. "Let's hope for better luck tomorrow."

Freddie watched as Brian picked up his backpack and walked out of the auditorium. "I want

27

to check out the place where Brian fell," Freddie told his twin.

Flossie nodded. "The floor wasn't slippery before."

As all the kids began to collect their things, the twins went up on the stage again. "This is where Brian fell," Freddie said, pointing.

"What's that shiny stuff?" Flossie asked.

Freddie crouched down and touched the wet-looking spot on the floor. Then he sniffed his fingers. "Floor wax," he whispered.

"What are you two doing up there?" Mr. Horton called out. "Didn't you hear Mrs. McKenna say that rehearsal is over?"

"We thought we'd check out the floor to see why Brian fell," Freddie explained.

"There's no need for that," said Mr. Horton. "Brian just slipped. Now, get off that stage right away."

"What a crab," Freddie whispered to Flossie.

The twins headed toward the door of the auditorium. Nan and Bert were waiting for them. Suddenly Flossie cried out, "My sweater! I left it backstage."

"Better go get it, Flossie," Nan told her.

Mr. Horton was standing at the door. "Please hurry," he said. "We all want to go home."

"See you tomorrow, Roy," Mrs. McKenna said to Mr. Horton as she walked out the door. "Good work, kids! You're all terrific, and the show is going to be great."

"Thanks, Mrs. McKenna," Bert said, holding the door open for her. Freddie noticed that Mr. Horton didn't say anything to Mrs. McKenna.

"Freddie, would you please see what your sister is doing back there?" Mr. Horton asked.

"Sure," Freddie said, hurrying backstage. He found Flossie kneeling in front of an open supply cabinet. "Come on, Flossie," he said. "Mr. Horton wants to lock up."

Flossie's blue eyes were shining with excitement. "Wait till you see what I just found!" she said. She pointed to a can of wax in the cabinet.

Freddie reached out for the can. "It's wet!" he said, pulling his hand back.

"We're waiting!" Mr. Horton called impatiently.

"Do you have your sweater?" Freddie asked.

"What sweater?" Flossie said. She looked confused.

"The sweater you left behind," Freddie reminded her.

"Oh, I don't have a sweater," Flossie told him. "I just said that so I could check out this cabinet. I remembered seeing it back here."

"Good work, Flossie," Freddie said as they headed back to the door. "My sister can't find her sweater," he told Mr. Horton.

"You can look for it tomorrow, Flossie," the teacher told her.

"Okay," Flossie agreed.

Once they were outside, Flossie told Nan and Bert what she had found. "Someone put wax on the floor on purpose," she said.

Nan frowned. "And it sure seems as if someone tampered with the rope, too."

"And don't forget the volume controls on our equipment," Bert added.

"I can't believe someone is trying to ruin the show," Nan said.

"I bet I know who it is," Freddie offered.

"Who?" Flossie asked excitedly.

"Danny Rugg, of course," Freddie said. He kicked at a pebble. "He always tries to ruin things."

"Speaking of Danny," Bert said. "There he is, at the corner."

"Maybe we can find out what's going on right now," Nan told the others. Then she shouted, "Hey, Danny! Wait up!"

Danny stopped walking and turned around as the Bobbseys ran up to him.

"I can't wait to hear you on the accordion tomorrow," Nan told him. "How long have you been playing?"

Danny looked at her suspiciously. "A while," he said. "I told my mother I wasn't going to take violin anymore, so she made me pick another instrument."

"Well, do you like the accordion?" Nan asked. She bent down to tie her shoe.

"Are you nuts?" Danny answered. "You think I *want* to be in a stupid PTA show?" He walked away, shaking his head.

Bert turned to Nan, who had just straightened up. "What was that all about?"

"He had spots on his sneakers!" Nan announced. "The spots could have been floor wax."

Bert shook his head. "Come on, Nan. Lots of people have spots on their sneakers."

Freddie looked down. His shoes had spots on them, all right.

Nan shrugged. "Yes, but he also said he doesn't want to be in the show. If the show was canceled, Danny would be happy."

"Good point," said Bert, nodding.

The next day Freddie was seated across from Mary Caldera in the school library. "I think the show should be canceled," Mary told him. "It's going to be terrible."

"No, it isn't," Freddie said. "Some of the acts are really good."

"Oh, your act with Teddy is okay," Mary said. "But those tap dancers are awful. And the Aliens are so loud."

Freddie decided not to argue with her even though he didn't agree.

"Actually," Mary went on, "I'm very upset

about my piano player, Andrea. I sing so much better than she plays. I asked some other kids if they would play for me, but they all said they were too busy."

"Let's keep our voices down, please," the librarian called out. Mary shrugged and opened the book in front of her.

Freddie looked down at his book, too. He was supposed to be working on a special project. But he was thinking about what Mary had said. No wonder no one wanted to play piano for her. She was really stuck-up.

Just then Flossie's voice came floating across the library. "Ms. Hanson asked me to get Freddie," she explained to the librarian. "One of the kids in our class is having a birthday party."

Freddie left the library with his sister. On the way back to their classroom they passed the teachers' lounge. Mr. Horton was standing inside, near the open door. The smell of fresh coffee drifted out of the lounge.

"The show?" the twins heard Mr. Horton say. "Please, don't ask!"

Flossie turned to Freddie and put her finger to her lips. They both stopped to listen.

"Some of the kids have talent, but they need good, firm direction. Teaching music doesn't make a person an expert on directing."

Freddie and Flossie exchanged looks. Mr. Horton had to be talking about Mrs. McKenna.

"And I should know," Mr. Horton went on. "I am a *real* director. The PTA should get rid of Nancy McKenna and let *me* whip that show into shape!"

5

More Disasters

"Mr. Horton wants to direct the show," Flossie whispered to Freddie. "Maybe he thinks the PTA will give him Mrs. McKenna's job if the show is in enough trouble."

Just then Mr. Horton came out into the hall. "Shouldn't you children be in class?" he asked the twins.

"We're on our way right now," Flossie said quickly. "Come on, Freddie."

Soon the twins were safe inside their own classroom. "I have the paper plates here," Ms. Hanson told the class. "But I must have left the cups in the office. Would you kids start pushing the desks together while I go get them?"

"Yes, Ms. Hanson," Flossie said.

Everyone began to push a long line of desks together. "Flossie, do you really think Mr. Horton would mess up the whole show just to make Mrs. McKenna look bad?" Freddie asked in a low voice.

"Sure," Flossie said. "Mr. Horton knows his way around the auditorium. I bet he knows which rope controls the cloth that fell on Mary Caldera. I bet he knows about the cabinet with the wax, too."

"A lot of people could know those things," Freddie said. "Danny Rugg was standing right near the rope, remember?"

"Yes," Flossie replied. "But I also remember who was standing not too far from Danny—Mr. Horton."

Freddie nodded. "Okay," he said. "You keep an eye on Danny today at rehearsal. I'll watch Mr. Horton."

* * *

When the twins arrived at rehearsal that afternoon, two older boys were telling jokes.

"Come on," Freddie said. "Teddy must be waiting for us."

Quietly Freddie and Flossie made their way down the side of the auditorium. They noticed that some kids were sitting in the front rows. Then the twins climbed the short flight of steps that led backstage.

"That was a pretty dumb joke, Keith," one of the boys onstage was saying to the other. "But your watermelon joke was even worse. It was really *pit*-i-ful."

Freddie and Flossie heard the kids in the audience groan. Then they heard Mrs. McKenna say, "Okay, fellas. We'll have to work on your timing. But I'm sure you'll do fine."

Freddie took off to find Teddy. Flossie spotted Danny Rugg leaning against a wall, playing a hand-held electronic game. She decided to stand where she could watch Danny *and* the rehearsal.

After the comedians had left the stage, Andrea Lee came running out. "Mrs. McKenna," she called. "We have a problem."

"Oh, dear." The director sighed. "What now?"

Next Mary Caldera stomped onto the stage. She looked furious. "Somebody stole my sheet music! Andrea left it backstage a few minutes ago, and now it's gone!"

"Oh, dear," Mrs. McKenna repeated. She stepped up to the edge of the stage. "Attention, everyone! Will you all please look around for Mary's music?"

Flossie glanced over at Danny Rugg. He was still leaning against the wall, and he was still playing his game. Flossie was pretty sure he hadn't taken the music. She looked around for Freddie.

She spotted him helping Teddy carry his equipment out from the dressing room backstage. Even though Freddie was supposed to be watching Mr. Horton, Flossie figured her twin hadn't had time to do much detective work.

"Is this what you're looking for?" Mr. Horton called. He was waving a sheaf of papers covered with music notes. "I found it on the floor."

"Oh, thank you," said Andrea, taking the music. For the first time Flossie saw her smile.

"This place is such a mess, it's no wonder things disappear," Mr. Horton said. He moved to one side of the stage.

"Then maybe you should do some cleaning up," Mrs. McKenna suggested. "Mary and Andrea, let's go through the song now."

Andrea played beautifully, but again Mary missed some of the notes. Flossie watched as Danny pretended to sing along with Mary, moving his lips and making funny faces.

"Danny Rugg! You're on!" Mrs. McKenna yelled after Mary had practiced taking about twenty bows. Danny grabbed his accordion case and dragged it onstage. "For the show, take out your instrument before you enter, Danny," Mrs. McKenna told him.

"Okay," Danny mumbled as he bent down to open the case. "Hey," he said angrily. "The lock is stuck!"

The kids in the audience watched Danny struggle to open his accordion case. Finally Bert jumped up onstage, holding his Rex Sleuther pocketknife. Using the pocketknife's miniature pliers, he opened the case. "There was a toothpick jamming the lock," Bert explained.

Danny gave Bert a dirty look. Then he picked up his accordion and began to play. To Flossie's surprise, he didn't sound half-bad.

When Danny was finished, Mrs. McKenna checked her list. "Brian Mueller, let's see your juggling act."

Brian walked out onstage and immediately dropped a juggling pin on his toe. He began hopping on one foot while moaning and holding his other foot. "I can't rehearse, Mrs. McKenna," Brian said. "My toe hurts too much."

Mrs. McKenna looked upset. "Oh, all right," she said. "Let's have Teddy Blake's magic act, then."

"There is absolutely no discipline here!" Mr. Horton burst out. "We have a show to put on tomorrow. This rehearsal is a zoo!"

Freddie handed Teddy's wand to Flossie. "Come on," he said. "We're on."

But as Flossie stepped toward the stage, she

heard Brian Mueller talking to Mary Caldera. "Your song is okay," he said. "But I'm going to be the star of the show."

"Oh, yeah?" Mary shot back. "Well, there can only be one star. And it's not going to be you, Brian—not if *I* can help it!"

6

New Wrinkles

"Maybe Mary's trying to get Brian upset so he'll bomb at the show tomorrow," Flossie told Freddie after rehearsal was over. They were standing in the school yard, waiting for Bert and Nan.

Freddie rolled his eyes. "Then why would she dump a curtain over her own head? Get real, Flossie."

Flossie bit her lip. "Good point. But Mary wasn't just bragging in there, Freddie! She was threatening Brian. I'm sure she's planning to cause trouble."

"Maybe," Freddie said. "But this whole thing has me stumped."

"Or Mr. Horton could be messing everything up," Flossie said. "He doesn't have a very good attitude, that's for sure."

"I didn't see him do anything suspicious this afternoon," Freddie pointed out. "It's funny how he found Mary's music, though. It sure didn't take him very long."

At that moment Brian came out of the auditorium door. He seemed worried and sad. If Mary was trying to upset Brian, Freddie thought, she was doing a great job.

Just then a car pulled up to the curb and honked its horn. Inside, Freddie saw a man and woman with gray hair waving at Brian. Brian ran to the car, opened the door, and hopped in.

"Ground Control to Freddie Bobbsey," a voice said in Freddie's ear.

Freddie jumped. Bert and Nan had come up behind him. "Hey, what kept you guys?" Freddie asked.

"We had to pack our equipment and put it away in the storage room," Nan replied.

As the twins were walking home, Freddie said, "I think Brian's grandparents are visiting him." He explained about the gray-haired man and woman in the car.

"Big deal," Flossie said. "What has that got to do with anything? Concentrate on the case, Freddie."

"Look, there's Brian now," said Bert. He pointed down the street.

Brian was standing in his driveway, juggling three rings. When he noticed the Bobbseys, he missed his next catch. The ring rolled down the driveway toward the street. Freddie caught it and tossed it back.

"Thanks," Brian said.

As they were talking, the woman with gray hair came out of the house. She was carrying a plate of cookies and a glass of milk.

"Here, sweetie sweet, I brought you a snack," she called. Then she noticed the twins. "Oh, I'm sorry, Brian," she said. "I didn't know your friends were here. I have more cookies in the kitchen."

"That's okay, thanks," Nan said quickly. "We're on our way home to dinner."

"I'm so glad to meet you," the woman said. "I'm Brian's grandmother."

Freddie shot a look of triumph at Flossie.

"Are you all in the talent show, too?" Brian's grandmother asked. The Bobbseys nodded. "Isn't that nice! I'm working on Brian's costume now. He'll be the cutest hobo you ever saw."

Brian's face, already pink from being called "sweetie sweet," turned bright red. "They'll see it tomorrow," he mumbled.

"Yes, of course, dear. And I know you'll be the star of the show. *One* of the stars, I mean," she added. She smiled at the Bobbseys.

"We'd better go," Bert said. "Nice to meet you." He and the other twins waved goodbye.

"I'll be watching for all of you tomorrow night," Brian's grandmother called after them.

The dress rehearsal for the show started right after school on Friday afternoon. Flossie changed into the black pants and turtleneck that she would be wearing in the show. Freddie's outfit matched hers. Magicians' assistants always wore black, Teddy had told them. That was so everyone would watch the magician.

Flossie waited while Nan put on her Alien costume—a tie-dyed T-shirt, electric blue leggings, and pink-and-purple sneakers. "You look pretty wild," Flossie observed.

"Thanks," said Nan. "That's the idea." They went into the auditorium. Bert was there, in black jeans and a vest painted with stars.

"Oh, good, you're all here," Mrs. McKenna said from the doorway. "Hello, Danny. What a terrific costume."

The twins turned around, and Danny scowled at them. He was wearing brown leather shorts with suspenders, a white shirt with embroidery, green knee socks, and a little hat with a feather pinned to one side. "These clothes are from Europe," he said. "They all dress like this over there. It's like a tradition."

A funny look crossed Mrs. McKenna's face, but she didn't say anything.

Bert and Nan went to find the rest of the Aliens. Freddie turned to Flossie. "That Brian is such a jerk," he said. "I was going to show him that great juggling trick I learned from Togo the Clown. It's a trick that takes two people. But Brian said he had all the tricks he needed."

"I guess he's just real nervous," Flossie said.

"Mrs. McKenna! Mrs. McKenna!" Brian rushed out to center stage. "The cassette my dad made for my act isn't in my bag!" he cried. "And I saw it there just a few minutes ago."

"Boy," Mary Caldera said to her friend Andrea. "Can you believe how many things have been going wrong around here?"

Brian looked around at the others. "You'd better all quit while you can," he said. "I know I'm going to. This show is jinxed!"

7

The Jinx Strikes Again

"Now, Brian," Mrs. McKenna said. "Let's not get carried away. We'll all help you look for your tape. Where did you see it last?"

"It was in my backpack when I came backstage," he said. "But when I took my costume out of the backpack just now, it wasn't there."

"Maybe it slipped underneath something," Nan suggested.

"Or got caught in your costume," Andrea spoke up. "I lose my barrettes that way all the time."

After a short search Flossie called out, "I found it!" She held up the plastic cassette case.

"Good for you, Flossie," Mrs. McKenna said. "Where was it?"

Flossie hesitated. "On the floor," she said. "Behind Danny's accordion case."

"What?" Danny exclaimed. "I bet you hid it there yourself, just to get me in trouble!"

"I did not," Flossie insisted. "I found it there, just like I said."

"What's going on here?" Mr. Horton appeared at the head of the steps that led onto the stage.

"Brian lost his music cassette," Mrs. McKenna explained. "And Flossie Bobbsey just found it."

Mr. Horton looked over at Brian. "One of the first rules of the theater is to take good care of your props," he said. "Remember that."

Mrs. McKenna glared at Mr. Horton. "There's another rule of the theater," she said. "Don't upset the performers just before opening night." She turned to Brian. "I'm sorry your tape got misplaced, Brian, but you have it back now. You'll stay in the show, won't you? I know

your family must be looking forward to seeing you tonight."

Brian looked down at the floor. "All right," he muttered. "But I still say the show is jinxed."

"As long as you give it your best shot, I'm sure you'll be fine," Mrs. McKenna told him. "Now, go get into your costume. Aliens, are you all set?"

"Two minutes," Nan called from the stage.

While Bert and Nan's band was hooking up its equipment, Flossie and Freddie went to a quiet corner of the auditorium to discuss the case.

"Who took Brian's tape?" asked Freddie. "Do you think it was Danny?"

"I don't know," Flossie replied. "The tape was by his accordion case, but Mary was standing near Brian's backpack. I didn't see her touch it, but she could have."

"Hmm," Freddie said. "Well, we can cross off Mr. Horton. He didn't even get here until after Brian's tape disappeared."

"Are you sure?" Flossie asked.

Freddie nodded. "There's no back door on that side of the stage. You have to go up the stairs from the auditorium to get there. And I was right by the stairs when Mr. Horton came up them. He couldn't have taken the tape."

"Rats," Flossie said. "I was hoping it was him. I think he's mean to Mrs. McKenna."

"I do, too," Freddie said. "But that doesn't mean that Mr. Horton is trying to wreck the show. I still think Danny's the one."

"I guess so," said Flossie. "But we should keep an eye on Mary, too. She'd do anything to make herself look better than everyone else. We heard her threatening Brian, remember? And Brian's had more dirty tricks played on him than anybody."

Freddie nodded. "Right. We'll have to watch both Mary and Danny. You take Mary, and I'll stick close to Danny. The minute either of them tries to pull another stunt, we'll have them."

Just then the side door of the auditorium opened. Brian's grandparents walked in and looked around. His grandmother spotted Freddie and Flossie and waved. Freddie waved back, then nudged Flossie. "Wave, sweetie sweet," he whispered. Flossie giggled and waved.

Brian's grandparents sat down, and Mrs. McKenna hurried over to them. "I'm sorry," she told them. "Nobody is allowed to watch the dress rehearsal."

"Oh, but we're so anxious to see our Brian," his grandmother protested.

"I'm afraid you'll have to wait till the show," Mrs. McKenna said gently. She walked the gray-haired man and woman out of the auditorium. When she came back, she was alone.

Freddie tapped Flossie on the arm. Then he nodded toward the front of the auditorium. Mary and Andrea were sitting in the first row. Mary was wearing her costume, a pink satin dress trimmed with white lace. Quickly Flossie went and sat behind the two girls as the Aliens began to play.

Freddie ran up the stairs at the side of the stage. Then he ducked behind the curtains. Danny was standing against a wall, playing his electronic game. Mrs. McKenna was sitting on a high stool near the light panel, studying her clipboard. In the corner Teddy was making a quarter appear and disappear.

Then Freddie saw Brian coming toward him. He was wearing patched, baggy pants with suspenders and a shirt that was way too big for him. He also had on a stiff brown hat and a big pair of old shoes. Under his arm he held a patched coat. "I'm a hobo," he told Freddie. "My grandmother thought it up."

"I know," Freddie replied.

"I wanted to wear all black, like you and Flossie," Brian continued. "That way the colors of the rings and the Indian clubs would have shown up better. But when Grandma gets an idea . . ."

"I know what you mean," Freddie said with a grin. "Are your grandparents here for long?"

Brian shook his head. "Just till Sunday. You're lucky you've got brothers and sisters. You don't have your whole family watching you all the time."

Freddie thought for a minute. "That's true," he said finally. "But sometimes, when I do something great, nobody notices."

"I never thought of that," Brian said.

Suddenly Freddie remembered that he was supposed to be watching Danny Rugg. "See you later," he told Brian quickly. "Good luck."

Danny was still in the same spot. Didn't he ever move? Freddie thought. Freddie went over and stood near him as the Aliens finished.

Just then Teddy ran up. "Where's Flossie?" he demanded. "Mrs. McKenna changed the program. She wants us to go on next!"

"I'll get her," Freddie replied. He went to the steps and beckoned to Flossie.

"Brian Mueller?" Mrs. McKenna called. "You're coming up soon, after Teddy and Mary."

"I'm just going to the water fountain," Brian replied. "I'll be right back."

In the front row Mary whispered something to Andrea. The two girls got up and walked toward the stage. Flossie was right behind them. "We can't watch our suspects while we're helping Teddy," Flossie told Freddie. "And there's no time to get Bert and Nan."

Freddie nodded. "We'll just have to keep our fingers crossed that nothing happens."

The twins and Teddy started their act. Suddenly an angry shout came from backstage.

Brian rushed out onto the stage in his bare feet. "My shoes!" he cried. "They're stuck to the floor!"

8

A Sticky Situation

Everyone ran backstage. Sure enough, there were Brian's big shoes.

Mrs. McKenna bent down and tugged at them. They were glued solidly to the floor. "Who is responsible for this?" she demanded angrily.

The giggling and whispers died away.

"I told you this show is jinxed," Brian mumbled.

"Don't be ridiculous!" Mrs. McKenna snapped. "A jinx didn't put glue on your shoes. Someone with a very sick sense of humor did. Here, let me see if I can pry them loose."

Mrs. McKenna went to the supply cabinet and came back with a paint scraper. She pushed the edge under one of the shoes and wiggled the scraper from side to side.

"There," she said when she'd managed to free both shoes. "Now, listen up, everybody. When I find out who pulled these pranks, he or she is going to be one sorry person. If there are any more pranks, I may even cancel the show!" She looked around at everyone. "Now can we please get on with the rehearsal? Whose turn is it? Mary?"

Freddie noticed that Mary had a tiny smile on her lips. "I'm ready," she told Mrs. McKenna.

"Come on," Flossie whispered to Freddie. "Let's go out in the hall.

"Freddie," Flossie said, once they had left the auditorium, "we blew it."

"Well, we had to do our magic act, didn't we?" Freddie asked.

"Yeah, but we should have asked Bert and Nan to help us while there was still time," Flossie replied.

"I guess." Freddie frowned. "Wait a minute,

Flossie. How could somebody glue those shoes when there were so many people backstage?"

Flossie thought hard. "Maybe everyone else was watching Teddy," she suggested. "Then whoever it was could have squirted some quick-drying glue on the floor and dropped the shoes on it."

"That would take guts," Freddie said. "What if people smelled the glue? Or if they just happened to turn around?"

From the hall the twins heard the final, strangled notes of "Do-Re-Mi." Flossie rolled her eyes. "You know, I wish Mary would choose another song."

Freddie and Flossie headed back into the auditorium and headed for the stage. Mary was just finishing her usual twenty bows. Then she sailed off, wearing a big phony smile.

"Give me a break," Freddie said, disgusted.

Brian stepped onstage next. He put his rings and balls on the floor and began juggling the red, blue, and yellow clubs.

"Yikes!" Freddie murmured. "His timing is way off."

The red club was coming down just out of Brian's reach. He made a desperate lunge for it, while tossing the yellow club high in the air. Suddenly both clubs were spinning out of control.

"Watch out!" Flossie called to the tap dancers, who were watching Brian's act from the other side of the stage.

The yellow pin bopped one of the dancers on the shoulder. "Ouch!" she cried.

"Sorry," Brian called, red-faced.

Freddie picked up the red club, which had fallen at his feet. He tossed it back to Brian. Brian put it down behind him and picked up the rings.

Some of the kids were giggling. For someone who had bragged so much about his juggling, Brian certainly looked clumsy. Even Mrs. McKenna was shaking her head.

"I feel sorry for Brian," Flossie told Freddie. "I can't believe someone glued his shoes to the floor. That must have really messed him up."

"Hi, everyone!" called a voice from the back of the auditorium. It was Mrs. Franklin, the PTA president. "I've brought some popcorn and juice, in case you're hungry."

Most of the kids raced down the steps of the stage. Mrs. Franklin was unloading an enormous shopping bag in one of the back rows.

"Thanks, Joy," Mrs. McKenna said. "We can all use a snack at this point."

"Popcorn!" Flossie said eagerly. "Come on, Freddie!"

"I'll be right there," Freddie said. "I want to check out Danny's accordion case."

Flossie nodded and headed for the snacks. Making sure no one was watching, Freddie went backstage and looked around for Danny's instrument case. If he found a tube of glue inside, he'd know for sure that Danny was their culprit.

Finally Freddie spotted the case. His heart was beating wildly as he knelt down and opened it. The shiny red accordion took up most of the space, but there was a little compartment on the side.

Freddie opened the compartment. Inside, he saw a pack of tissues, a roll of candy, and thirty-five cents. No glue.

"Hey, squirt!" A hand grabbed Freddie's collar. "What are you doing with my stuff?" It was Danny, and he looked mad.

"I was just—" Freddie began. What could he say? I was looking for a tube of glue?

"You little twerp!" Danny scowled, pulling Freddie closer. Danny looked as if he was about to punch him in the face.

Just then Mrs. McKenna called, "Danny Rugg! Can we run through your number quickly, please?" Danny hesitated.

Freddie opened his mouth to holler for help. But at that moment all the lights in the auditorium went out!

Freddie tried to make out Danny's form in the pitch darkness. He reached out a hand.

Then he froze as he heard a strangled cry.

"Yeeeooowwww!"

9

Somebody's Got a Secret

A babble of frightened voices filled the darkness. "Keep calm, everybody," Mrs. McKenna called. "We'll have the lights working in a few seconds."

Danny let go of Freddie's shirt. Freddie slipped away from him and tried to remember where things were backstage. The master light switch was on a wall near the front of the stage. But which way was the front?

Freddie took a small, cautious step forward. Then he took another, waving his hands in front of him. His right hand bumped the wall. The switch must be nearby, Freddie thought. He ran his fingertips along the cinder-block wall.

Finally his knuckles rapped the side of the switchbox. He found the switch and flipped it on. Brian was sitting in the middle of the floor backstage. He was holding one elbow.

"Freddie Bobbsey!" Mrs. McKenna said angrily. She was standing at the top of the steps. "Did you turn the lights off?"

"No, I turned them back on," Freddie replied.

Then Mrs. McKenna noticed Brian. "What's the matter?" she asked him. "Did you hurt yourself again?"

"Somebody twisted my arm, after the lights went out," Brian said. "My elbow really hurts. That's why I screamed. Now I *know* I can't be in the show."

"This is the limit!" exclaimed Mrs. McKenna. "Okay, everybody, out front, right now!"

Freddie joined Flossie, Bert, Nan, and all the other performers in the auditorium. "What happened?" Flossie asked him.

"I'll tell you later," he replied.

Mrs. McKenna stood in front of the stage. "I am *very* upset by what's been going on," she said. "I want us to have a good time and put on a great show. Most of you want the same thing. But someone has been trying to ruin this project for all of us. I don't have any idea who or why. But if there's any more trouble, I'm going to call off the show."

"You can't do that!" Mr. Horton cried from the back of the auditorium. Then he rushed toward the stage.

Mrs. McKenna straightened her shoulders. "Oh, yes, I can. And I will, too. It's not too late. I'm not going to risk having anybody hurt by one of these so-called jokes. I'm sure the PTA will understand. Now, does anybody have anything to say?"

Danny got to his feet. Flossie looked at Nan. Was Danny about to confess?

"Yeah, I do," Danny said. "Any more trouble, and I'm going to get mad. I didn't spend all that time learning 'When the Swallows Come Back to Capistrano' just to have the show canceled."

"Why, thank you, Danny," Mrs. McKenna

said in a surprised voice. "Okay, that's it for my lecture. Danny, I think you're next."

While Danny was getting his accordion, the twins went over to Mrs. McKenna.

"We think we can find out who's causing the trouble," said Bert.

Mrs. McKenna raised her eyebrows. "That's right," she said slowly. "I've heard that you Bobbseys are terrific detectives."

"If we solve the case, will you let the show go on?" asked Flossie.

"Why, of course," Mrs. McKenna replied. "I don't *want* to cancel the show. But you'll have to work fast. There isn't much time. And the very next time anything happens, that's *it*."

"We'll do our best," Nan promised.

The twins gathered in a corner near the stage. "It wasn't Mary," Flossie said. "She was reaching for the popcorn when the lights went out. I was right next to her."

"And Danny was twisting the collar of my shirt," Freddie said. "He couldn't have been twisting Brian's arm at the same time."

"Who's left?" asked Bert. "Mr. Horton?"

"He was sitting at the back of the auditorium, taking notes," Nan said.

"Could he have slipped up onto the stage when you weren't looking?" Bert asked.

"He couldn't have slipped past me and Danny," Freddie replied. "Nobody could have. We were blocking the way backstage. It would have been impossible."

Flossie shut her eyes very tight. An idea had just popped into her head. "Wait a minute," she said. "There *is* one person who could have done it."

"Who, Flossie?" the others all asked at once.

"Follow me," Flossie said. "We have to get backstage before it's too late."

The twins tiptoed up the steps and ducked behind the curtain. Danny was still playing "When the Swallows Come Back to Capistrano."

It was crowded backstage. Mr. Horton was guarding the master light switch. Mary and Andrea were standing together, whispering. Teddy was showing Jimmy Pendleton one of his card tricks. In one corner Brian was folding up his hobo costume. His backpack was open on the floor next to him.

"Hi," Flossie said, walking up to him. "How does your arm feel?"

Brian looked miserable. "It hurts," he said. "A lot."

"You must be pretty disappointed about tonight," Flossie said. She moved a little closer to Brian, and he took a step backward. Suddenly Freddie realized what his twin was up to. He glanced at Bert and Nan. They looked as if they had caught on, too.

"It's too bad you won't be able to do your act," Flossie continued. Brian took another step backward. "After all your practicing and that special costume your grandmother made . . ."

As Brian backed away, Freddie glanced into his backpack. "Look!" he shouted. He bent down and pulled out a little tube. "Super Glue!"

Brian's mouth dropped open, but no words came out. He ran toward Freddie, but he was too late. Freddie had already pulled something else out of the backpack—a book.

"Hey," Freddie said, "I have this same book at

home. *How to Juggle in Ten Easy Steps.* Why didn't you tell anyone that you didn't know how to juggle? It isn't a crime."

"No, it isn't," Flossie said, folding her arms. "But some of the other stuff you pulled comes pretty close, Brian Mueller."

10

Encore!

"I didn't do anything!" Brian insisted.

"Come on, Brian," Freddie said. "You might as well admit the truth."

Brian bit his lip. "I wish I'd never been in this stupid show," he blurted out. "Now everyone is going to hate me."

"Nobody hates you, Brian," Flossie said. A group of kids had come up behind them.

Nan turned around. "Could you leave us alone for a minute, please?" she asked.

Mrs. McKenna and Mr. Horton appeared, too. "All right, kids, back to your places," Mrs. McKenna said to the crowd.

"This is a good time to check your props and costumes, anyway," Mr. Horton added.

Mrs. McKenna walked up to Brian and put a hand on his shoulder. "Brian, would you like to tell us what happened?"

Brian squeezed his eyes shut, and a big tear rolled down his face. "I told my grandparents I was a really great juggler," he said. "But it wasn't true. And I didn't think they'd come all the way from Florida to see me perform! I had to do something to get out of the show."

"You can't juggle at all?" Freddie asked.

Brian shook his head. "At first I thought I could learn real quick. But juggling is harder than it looks."

"So that's why you made all that trouble during rehearsals?" Mrs. McKenna asked.

Brian nodded sadly.

"Do you realize that someone might have been seriously injured?" Mr. Horton scolded. "What about that pole that almost fell on Mary Caldera?"

"I didn't make the pole fall, Mr. Horton,"

Brian insisted. "Honest! That really was an accident."

"Well, did you pour wax on the floor?" Mr. Horton asked. "And hide Mary's music and steal your own cassette? How about Danny Rugg's accordion case? Were you the one who jammed it?"

Brian nodded. "I also fiddled with the Aliens' equipment. I thought it would look weird if things happened only to me." He hung his head. "My grandparents think I'm so great," he said. "They don't know what a jerk I really am."

"You do know that we almost canceled the show because of your antics, don't you?" Mr. Horton said.

Mrs. McKenna flashed him a warning look. "That's enough, Roy. Brian is being very brave now by telling the truth."

"I'm really sorry," Brian said. His voice cracked. "Well, I'd better go home now."

Brian shrank away from Mrs. McKenna and walked over to his backpack.

"Wait, Brian," Mrs. McKenna said. "Let's see

if we can think of another solution to this problem," she said.

"I have an idea," Flossie volunteered. She turned to Freddie. "Remember the trick that Togo the Clown taught you? The one you were going to teach Brian?"

Freddie nodded. "Sure," he said. "It's really easy. If Brian and I can practice for a few minutes, I know he'll be able to learn it."

"How can I learn to juggle that fast?" Brian said. "I'm a total klutz!"

Mrs. McKenna put her hands on her hips. "Now, listen, Brian," she said firmly. "The least you can do is *try* to learn it." She checked her watch. "Better get busy, you two. The curtain goes up in about two hours!"

At seven o'clock that evening the Lakeport Elementary auditorium was packed. Backstage the performers were busy getting ready for the show. A few of them huddled at the edge of the stage, sneaking peeks at the crowd from behind the thick curtain.

"I see Mom and Dad!" Flossie told Nan excitedly.

Mrs. McKenna was shaking hands with well-wishers in front of the stage. Mrs. Franklin and the two school principals stood nearby, smiling.

"This is really exciting," Nan said. She looked fantastic in her Alien costume and makeup. "Half the town must have turned out for the show."

Soon Mrs. McKenna began to play "There's No Business Like Show Business" on the piano. That was the signal that the show was about to start.

"Take your places, everyone!" Mr. Horton said. "We're about to raise the curtain!"

Five tap dancers wearing short skirts and leotards took their places in the middle of the stage.

Soon the music stopped. From behind the curtain, the kids heard Mrs. Franklin greet the audience.

"Our performers have worked very hard," the PTA president said. "And so have the teachers,

Mrs. McKenna and Mr. Horton. Thanks for coming, and enjoy the show!"

Finally the curtain rose. The big show was on!

The tap-dancing number got things off to a great start. Teddy's magic act was a smash, too. The crowd cheered and whistled when it was over.

"Phew," Flossie said to Freddie as they came offstage. "We made it."

"Well, that's one down, one to go for me," Freddie said. "I'd better find Brian."

"Good luck," Flossie told him as he hurried backstage.

Mary Caldera was next. For the first time ever, she hit the right notes in her song. The audience applauded politely, all through her twenty bows.

Then came Danny Rugg. He was so nervous that Mr. Horton had to push him onto the stage. As soon as he stepped out, the audience laughed. Flossie guessed it was because of his costume. Still, at the end of Danny's song, there was a big burst of applause.

"Piece of cake," Danny said when he came offstage.

After Danny came the Aliens, and the crowd went wild. When the band had left the stage, Brian and Freddie came up beside Flossie. Brian looked nervous. "I can't do it!" he whispered to Freddie.

"Sure you can," said Freddie. "Let's go." The two of them ran out onto the stage as the audience clapped.

Brian was holding the rings and clubs, and Freddie had the balls. Looking very confident, Brian put down the clubs. Then he turned and tossed one of the rings to Freddie. Freddie dropped the balls to catch the ring. The balls bounced all over the stage. Then Brian tossed another ring to Freddie and bent down to pick up one of the balls.

At first the audience was silent, sure that the boys were making a mistake. Then some of the people started to laugh. Soon the whole crowd realized that Freddie and Brian were being clumsy on purpose. They began laughing and clapping, as more and more balls and rings started flying in every direction.

Freddie gave Brian a quick nod. Brian stuck his right hand in the air, and Freddie sailed the rings at it, one by one. This time he didn't miss. As the rings settled over Brian's arm, Freddie quickly picked up the balls. Then the two of them met in the middle of the stage and bowed.

Big cheers filled the auditorium like a wave. Freddie saw Brian's grandparents in the front row. They were on their feet, clapping and beaming with pride. Brian raised his arm to wave to them. The rings slid off and went rolling across the stage. The laughter and cheers were louder than ever.

"Thanks, Freddie," Brian said when they walked offstage. "I owe you one."

"No problem," Freddie told him with a grin.

The show continued. Veronica's violin playing was a hit. Keith and Pete's jokes were all funny. By the end of the show everyone knew it had been a big success. The whole cast came out to take a bow. When the curtain closed, Mrs. McKenna came backstage and gathered all the performers. "You gave a terrific show," she told them.

"Three cheers for Mrs. McKenna!" Mr. Horton said. Everybody cheered.

The director's face turned pink. "Thank you," she said. "And Mr. Horton deserves applause, too." There was more clapping.

"I guess I was wrong about a lot of things," Mr. Horton told Mrs. McKenna. "You really did a great job directing."

"Why, thank you, Roy," Mrs. McKenna said.

"Kids! You were marvelous!" gushed Mrs. Franklin as she stepped backstage. "This show has been the PTA's best fund-raiser yet! And I never would have guessed it after I saw your first rehearsal."

"Well, you know what they say," Mrs. McKenna said. She winked at Brian and the Bobbseys. "It's not how you start that counts. It's how you finish!"

NANCY DREW® MYSTERY STORIES By Carolyn Keene